DREAMWORKS

OFFICIAL HANDBOOK

ISBN 978-1-338-19656-6

10 9 8 7 6 5 4 3 2   17 18 19 20 21

Printed in the U.S.A.   40
First printing 2017

DREAMWORKS

CAPTAIN UNDERPANTS
THE FIRST EPIC MOVIE

OFFICIAL HANDBOOK

BY
KATE HOWARD

SCHOLASTIC INC.

THE
AMAZING
CAPTAIN
UNDERPANTS

CONTENTS

MEET GEORGE

This is George Beard and Harold Hutchins. George is the kid on the left with the tie and the flat-top. Harold is the one on the right with the T-shirt and the bad haircut.

Remember that now.

GEORGE BEARD

AND HAROLD

HAROLD
HUTCHINS

GEORGE AND HAROLD ARE FUN-LOVING BEST FRIENDS WHO SOMETIMES GET INTO A BIT OF TROUBLE. THEY DON'T *MEAN* TO CAUSE TROUBLE. THEY ARE JUST VERY FOND OF SILLY JOKES AND PRANKS. (IN CASE YOU DIDN'T ALREADY KNOW THIS, NOT EVERYONE LIKES PRANKS. OR JOKES. OR SILLINESS.) SOMETIMES, THE MISCHIEF GEORGE AND HAROLD MAKE LEADS TO BIG TROUBLE.

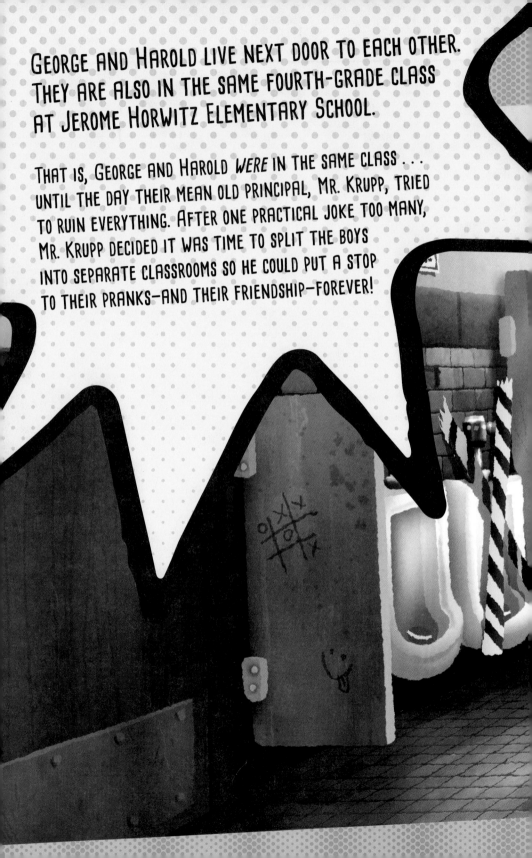

GEORGE AND HAROLD LIVE NEXT DOOR TO EACH OTHER. THEY ARE ALSO IN THE SAME FOURTH-GRADE CLASS AT JEROME HORWITZ ELEMENTARY SCHOOL.

THAT IS, GEORGE AND HAROLD *WERE* IN THE SAME CLASS . . . UNTIL THE DAY THEIR MEAN OLD PRINCIPAL, MR. KRUPP, TRIED TO RUIN EVERYTHING. AFTER ONE PRACTICAL JOKE TOO MANY, MR. KRUPP DECIDED IT WAS TIME TO SPLIT THE BOYS INTO SEPARATE CLASSROOMS SO HE COULD PUT A STOP TO THEIR PRANKS—AND THEIR FRIENDSHIP—FOREVER!

BUT BEFORE I CAN TELL YOU THAT STORY,
I HAVE TO TELL YOU *THIS* STORY . . .

The only thing George and Harold like more than practical jokes is creating comic books. The boys spend almost all their free time hanging out in the tree house between their backyards. Inside, they have two big fluffy chairs, a table, a cupboard stuffed with junk food, and a crate filled with pencils, pens, and stacks of paper.

All kinds of comic magic happens in George and Harold's headquarters. They spend hours writing and drawing comic books and trying to make each other laugh. Together, they have created hundreds of stories, all starring their own original superheroes.

I bet you're wondering if you've ever heard of any of their superheroes. Well, guess what? I'm getting to that. In case you can't wait any longer, here's a hint: Their greatest creation of all time is a superhero called THE AMAZING CAPTAIN UNDERPANTS.

CAPTAIN UNDERPANTS: THE ORIGIN ISSUE

A LONG, LONG, LONG, LONG TIME AGO IN A GALAXY FAR, FAR AWAY . . . THERE WAS A PLANET CALLED UNDERPANTYWORLD.

UNDERPANTYWORLD WAS A PEACEFUL PLANET WHERE EVERYBODY WORE ONLY UNDERWEAR . . . UNTIL IT STARTED TO BLOW UP FOR SOME REASON.

THE LEADERS OF UNDERPANTYWORLD SAVED THEIR BABY BY STRETCHING HIS UNDERWEAR REALLY FAR, AND THEN THEY SHOT HIM INTO SPACE. HE CRASHED ON EARTH, WHERE HE WAS RAISED BY SOME NICE FARM . . . DOLPHINS.

THE SPACE BABY GREW UP FAST . . . AND BECAME CAPTAIN UNDERPANTS!

GEORGE BEARD

(the one with the tie and the flat-top)

GEORGE BEARD WRITES THE STORIES FOR ALL OF HIS AND HAROLD'S COMIC BOOKS. BESIDES MAKING COMICS, HE ENJOYS SKATEBOARDING, WATCHING TV, PLAYING VIDEO GAMES, PULLING PRANKS, AND SAVING THE WORLD.

GEORGE IS CLEVER AND FUNNY, AND HIS SMARTS COME IN *VERY* HANDY WHEN HE AND HAROLD NEED TO TRICK SUPER-VILLAINS, OR WHEN IT'S TIME TO PULL PRANKS (LIKE REARRANGING CAFETERIA MENU LETTERS)!

GEORGE IS THE ONE WHO DISCOVERS THE HYPNO-RING—AND HE'S THE FIRST ONE TO WIELD IT.

ALL ABOUT GEORGE

Age: 9 ¾
Grade: Fourth
Favorite Food: Chocolate chip cookies
Pets: Two cats, Porky and Buckwheat

HAROLD HUTCHINS

(the one with the T-shirt and the bad haircut)

HAROLD HUTCHINS LOVES TO DRAW AND ILLUSTRATES ALL THE CAPTAIN UNDERPANTS ADVENTURES, AS WELL AS ALL THE OTHER COMICS HE AND GEORGE CREATE. WHEN HE'S NOT MAKING COMICS, HE CAN USUALLY BE FOUND DRAWING OR READING COMICS. HE ALSO ENJOYS SKATEBOARDING, PLAYING VIDEO GAMES, AND JAPANESE MONSTER MOVIES.

EVEN THOUGH HIS TEACHERS ALWAYS ORDER HIM TO STOP DOODLING, HAROLD'S CREATIVITY AND IMAGINATION OFTEN HELP HIM SAVE THE DAY. HE IS A TRUE EXPERT AT COMING UP WITH CLEVER PRANKS.

ALL ABOUT HAROLD

Age: 10
Grade: Fourth
Favorite Food: Gum
Pets: Five goldfish
named Moe, Larry,
Curly, Dr. Howard, and
Superfang

JEROME HORWITZ ELEMENTARY SCHOOL

SCHOOL RULES

No Pranks

No Jokes

No Yawning

No Breathing

No Smiling

No Fun

MEAN OLD MR. KRUPP

This old guy looking angry right here? That's Mr. Krupp, the worst principal in the world. Mean old Mr. Krupp hates everything fun: comic books, recess, kittens, even children. And he *especially* hates George and Harold!

I am going to annihilate your friendship. You won't be together. You won't be able to enjoy each other's company and ruin my life!

29

THE HYPNO-RING

After Mr. Krupp vows to destroy George and Harold's friendship, the two pranksters pull the ultimate stunt. Using a Hypno-Ring George found in a box of cereal, they hypnotize their principal and make him believe he's actually their superhero creation: CAPTAIN UNDERPANTS.

THIS SUPERPOWERED CRIME FIGHTER APPEARS WHEN ANYONE SNAPS THEIR FINGERS, AND THEN TURNS BACK INTO PRINCIPAL KRUPP WHEN HE GETS SPLASHED WITH WATER. WITH ONE SIMPLE SNAP OF THEIR FINGERS— *TRA-LA-LAAAAA!*—ALL OF GEORGE AND HAROLD'S PROBLEMS WITH MR. KRUPP DISAPPEAR!

THE HYPNO-RING

Forged from molten plastic in the lowest floor of the darkest basement where only toy prizes dare be made, it's the most powerful item ever to be found in a box of Frosted Sugar Doodles: the Hypno-Ring!

With this ring, you can have the power to amaze your friends, control your enemies, and take over the world!

FLIP-O-RAMA™!

The following pages contain scenes that are so intense and horrific . . .

. . . that we can only show it using a technology called FLIP-O-RAMA™!

How to Do Flip-O-Rama™

STEP 1: Place your *LEFT* hand inside the dotted lines marked "LEFT HAND HERE." Hold the book open *FLAT*.

STEP 2: Grasp the *RIGHT-HAND* page with your right thumb and index finger (inside the dotted lines marked "RIGHT THUMB HERE.").

STEP 3: Now *QUICKLY* flip the right-hand page back and forth until the picture appears to be *ANIMATED*.

LEFT HAND HERE

RIGHT
THUMB
HERE

When I snap my fingers, you will obey our every command.

39

CAPTAIN UNDERPANTS

WEARING TIGHTY-WHITIES, A RED CAPE, AND NOTHING ELSE,
CAPTAIN UNDERPANTS IS:

FASTER THAN A SPEEDING WAISTBAND,
MORE POWERFUL THAN BOXER SHORTS,
AND ABLE TO LEAP TALL BUILDINGS WITHOUT GETTING A WEDGIE!

Tra-La-
LAAAAA!

42

CAPTAIN UNDERPANTS

Night and day, Captain Underpants watches over the city, fighting for Truth, Justice, and all that is Pre-Shrunk and Cottony!

45

UNFORTUNATELY, THE WAISTBAND WARRIOR CAUSES A WHOLE NEW SET OF PROBLEMS WHEN HE TURNS JEROME HORWITZ ELEMENTARY SCHOOL INTO A RULE-FREE ZONE WHERE WHOOPEE CUSHIONS AND SPITBALLS RUN THE SHOW.

TO MAKE MATTERS WORSE: WHILE CAPTAIN UNDERPANTS IS CALLING THE SHOTS, GEORGE AND HAROLD CONVINCE HIM TO HIRE A NEW SCIENCE TEACHER, PROFESSOR P., AS A GAG . . . ONLY TO LEARN THAT THE *P* STANDS FOR POOPYPANTS AND HE'S A MAN WITH A NASTY PLAN!

47

PROFESSOR P. POOPYPANTS

Professor P. Poopypants is a brilliant scientist with a very silly name. Professor P. loves inventing . . . but he hates when people laugh at his name. Though Poopypants is a traditional name in the professor's home country, New Swissland, it's nothing more than a joke everywhere else in the world.

Many years ago, Professor Poopypants won the Nobel Peace Prize in Inventing Stuff for one of his greatest creations, the Sizerator 2000. With a single blast, this giant laser had the power to smallify or largify *anything*.

Receiving the prize should have been Professor P.'s proudest moment. But instead of applause, the only thing the esteemed professor heard was *laughter*. Everyone was laughing at his name!

After years of hard work, Professor P. has finally come up with a plan to rid the world of laughter—forever and ever. Though he has no teaching experience, he gets a job as the new science teacher at Jerome Horwitz Elementary School. He believes that as long as kids do not laugh, smile, or play, they're just peachy.

Hiya, class! I'm your cool, new teacher! Not some scary guy with a secret, evil agenda . . .

Oh, this is bad. We just hired a maniac for a science teacher!

MELVIN SNEEDLY

Anti-Humor Boy

MELVIN SNEEDLY IS A KNOW-IT-ALL ABOUT *EVERYTHING* . . . EXCEPT HAVING FUN. THIS SNEAKY, NO-FUN TATTLETALE LOVES NOTHING MORE THAN GETTING HAROLD AND GEORGE IN TROUBLE WITH PRINCIPAL KRUPP.

MELVIN NEVER APPRECIATES ANY OF HIS CLASSMATES' PRANKS. HIS LACK OF HUMOR HAS NEVER BEEN A *REAL* PROBLEM BEFORE . . . BUT HIS MISSING HUMOR GENE CAUSES BIG TROUBLE WHEN PROFESSOR POOPYPANTS COMES TO JEROME HORWITZ ELEMENTARY SCHOOL.

I don't get it. Why is it funny?!

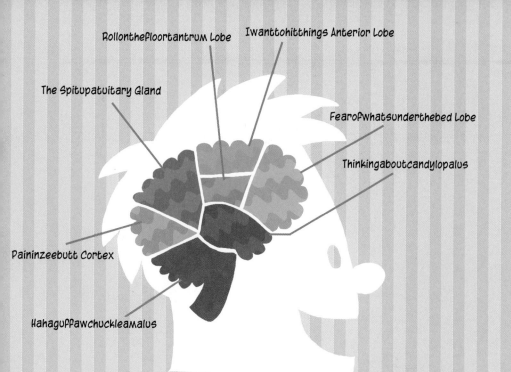

Rollonthefloortantrum Lobe

Iwanttohitthings Anterior Lobe

The Spitupatuitary Gland

Fearofwhatsunderthebed Lobe

Thinkingaboutcandylopalus

Paininzeebutt Cortex

Hahaguffawchuckleamalus

Zee Brain of Zee Average Child

PROFESSOR POOPYPANTS WANTS TO RID THE WORLD OF LAUGHTER. ACCORDING TO PROFESSOR P., THE HAHAGUFFAWCHUCKLEAMALUS IS THE PART OF THE BRAIN THAT GIVES YOU THE POWER TO LAUGH. THIS FUNNY LITTLE PURPLE LOBE HOLDS A PERSON'S ENTIRE CAPACITY FOR LAUGHTER.

FOR YEARS, PROFESSOR P. TRIED TO FIND SOME WAY TO SHRINK OR CUT OUT THE HAHAGUFFAWCHUCKLEAMALUS ENTIRELY ... BUT HE NEVER FIGURED IT OUT. UNTIL HE MET MELVIN SNEEDLY, WHO WAS BORN WITHOUT ONE—MAKING HIM THE PERFECT PARTNER FOR THE EVIL PROFESSOR'S PERILOUS PLOT!

THE TURBO TOILET 2000

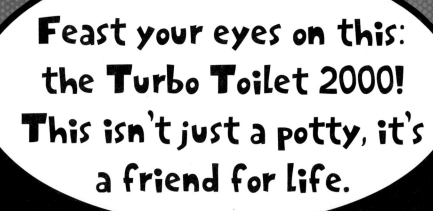

Feast your eyes on this: the **Turbo Toilet 2000**! This isn't just a potty, it's a friend for life.

THE TURBO TOILET 2000 WAS ONE OF MELVIN'S INVENTION CONVENTION CREATIONS. BUT WHEN PROFESSOR POOPYPANTS GETS HIS HANDS ON IT, HE CRANKS—ER, *FLUSHES*—THIS POTTY UP A NOTCH.

THE TURBO TOILET 2000

Filled with toxic goo and controlled by the evil Professor P., this majestic potty towers over every other structure in town. The mighty toilet gives Professor Poopypants the muscle he needs to carry out his war on laughter and his arch-enemy nemesis: the amazing Captain Underpants!

THE PERILOUS PLOT OF PROFESSOR POOPYPANTS

The epic battle is on! Will the Briefs of Justice prevail over the maniacal mad scientist and his toxic toilet?

HERE WE GO AGAIN!